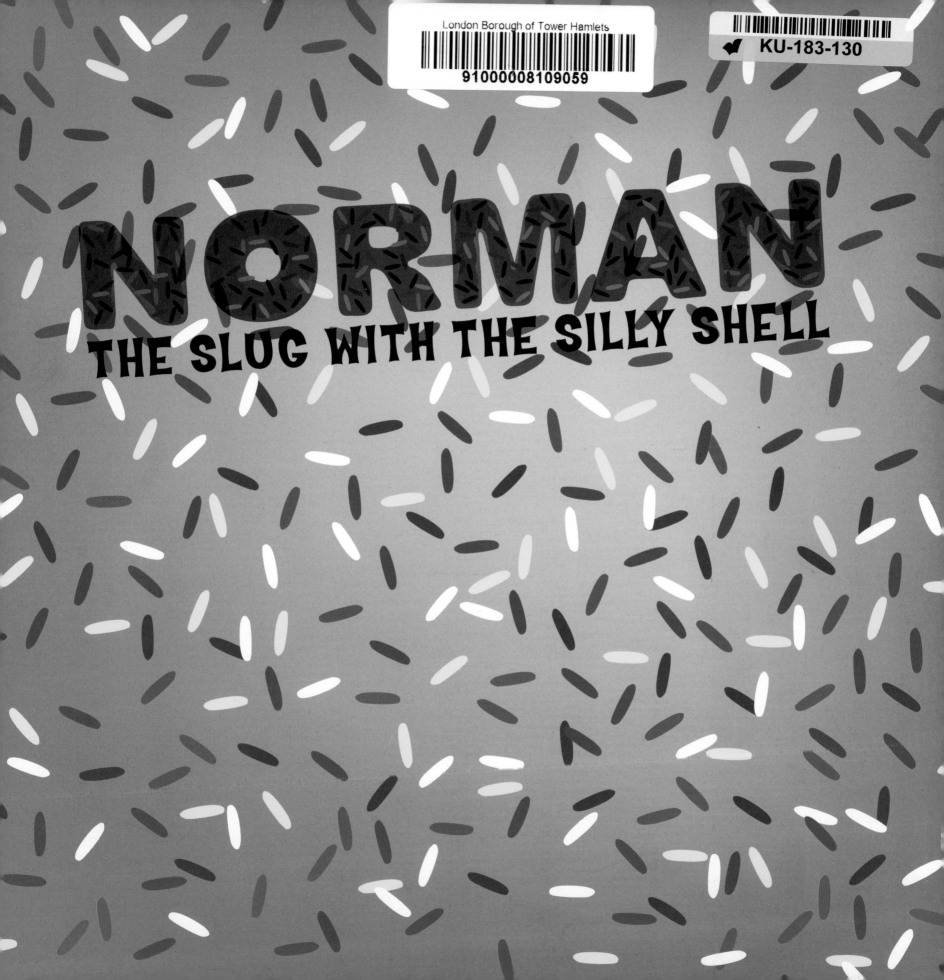

NORMAN
THE SLUG WITH THE SILLY SHELL

Meet Sue and Paul:

Sue Hendra and **Paul Linnet** have been making books together since 2009 when they came up with *Barry the Fish with Fingers*, and since then they haven't stopped. If you've ever wondered which one does the writing and which does the illustrating, wonder no more . . . they both do both!

For Rosa

SIMON & SCHUSTER

First published in Great Britain in 2011 • This edition published in 2021 by Simon & Schuster UK Ltd
1st Floor, 222 Gray's Inn Road, London, WC1X 8HB
Text and illustrations copyright © 2011, 2021 Sue Hendra and Paul Linnet
The right of Sue Hendra and Paul Linnet to be identified as the authors and illustrators of this work
has been asserted by them in accordance with the Copyright, Designs and Patents Act, 1988
All rights reserved, including the right of reproduction in whole or in part in any form
A CIP catalogue record for this book is available from the British Library upon request
978-1-4711-9740-6 • Printed in China • 10 9 8 7 6 5 4 3 2 1

NORMAN
THE SLUG WITH THE SILLY SHELL

by Sue Hendra
and Paul Linnet

SIMON & SCHUSTER
London   New York   Sydney
Toronto   New Delhi

Norman the slug thought snails were great.
"Wow!" said Norman. "Look at them! They're amazing!"

But, unfortunately, the snails didn't think Norman was great.

WHEE!

CRASH!

"Norman, you silly slug!" they cried. "You've spoilt our fun. This only works if you've got a shell."

Norman felt left out. Sadly, he skulked off into the moonlight.

"If only I had a shell of my own," he sighed,
looking at his reflection.

And that's when he had an idea!
"Maybe I could have a shell after all,"
he thought.

But finding a shell was not as easy as it seemed.

One was too bouncy,

one was too NOISY,

and one was already taken!

Norman needed time to think . . .

Ta-da!
A shell!

It was perfect!

Norman had never been happier.
He could join the snails at last.

Norman LOVED being a snail.

And the snails LOVED Norman's silly shell.

But the fun didn't last for long.

Suddenly, there was a loud flapping of wings.

"Look out! Bird!" cried the snails in panic.
"Quick, slither for your lives or we'll end up as supper!"

But the bird was more interested in Norman's silly shell – it looked DELICIOUS!

Norman was being carried up, up and away, higher and higher into the sky.

What could he do?

Norman did the only thing a slug could do.
He made slime – lots and lots of it!

With a slither and a slother, a slip and a slide,
Norman was FREE!

But he was falling

faster and

faster and

FASTER until . . .

PLONK!

"Norman, Norman, are you OK?"
asked the snails.

"Wow!" said Norman. "That was great.
I LOVE flying. If only I had wings . . ."

Ta-da!

If you like

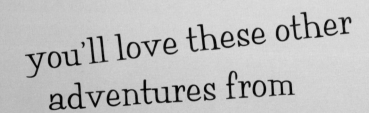

NORMAN
THE SLUG WITH THE SILLY SHELL

you'll love these other
adventures from

Sue Hendra and
Paul Linnet

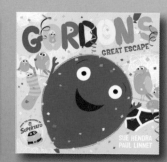